Melissa Madenski

SOME OF THE PIECES

Illustrated by Deborah Kogan Ray

Z I5I75

7/93

Little, Brown and Company

Boston Toronto London

First Edition

Library of Congress Cataloging-in-Publication Data
Madenski, Melissa.
    Some of the pieces / by Melissa Madenski; illustrated by Deborah
Kogan Ray. — 1st ed.
        p. cm.
    Summary: A year after the death of the father, two children and their
mother try to come to terms with their loss.
    ISBN 0-316-54324-1
    [1. Death—Fiction. 2. Fathers—Fiction. 3. Grief—Fiction.]   I. Ray,
Deborah Kogan, 1940– ill.   II. Title.
    PZ7.M25648So   1991
    [E]—dc20   90-46964

10 9 8 7 6 5 4 3 2 1

Imago

Published simultaneously in Canada
by Little, Brown & Company (Canada) Limited

Printed in Hong Kong

For Mark
— M. M.

For Diana and John
— D. K. R.

It has been a year since my dad died. Today we're going to the river to throw the last of his ashes into the water. We walk across slimy mud that grabs at our feet—my baby sister calls it "mucky-muck." Mom carries her across the parts where old river water oozes around our toes.

We walk to where the river meets the ocean and find some smooth, round rocks to stand on. "This is the perfect place to rest," says my mother.

Mom and I share stories about Dad while my sister throws ashes and dances around and around at the river's edge.

We build tunnels in the sand and wade in the river. My mom leans on me to take her shoes off. "You're getting as tall and slim as those birds out there," she says, looking at the herons fishing in the river. "But I remember when you were only a little bigger than the hammer your father used to build houses."

I've heard lots of stories about when I was a baby. My dad told me how he gave me baths in a white porcelain tub on the dining-room table. "Your hands were closed, as if you were holding something," he said.

"We listened to cello music," he told me. "Your arms floated up and down—you looked like a bird drifting lazily on the wind." He had called to my mother, "This is a baby who likes music!"

It's time to go home. We walk up the steep road to our car. My sister rides on Mom's back, and I carry the beach toys and buckets. As I brush a fly off my ear, some sand falls on my feet.

"When you were two, you called Dad 'Papa,'" Mom says.

"And he always called me 'Bubbo,' right?" I ask her.

Mom nods and smiles.

When I ask her why, she says, "No particular reason. He liked the sound of it."

When I step into the car, I bump my sister with the buckets. She makes a face at me but lets me buckle her seatbelt. She lays her head against my arm. Her face feels hot, and her hair smells like the river.

"I remember sitting on the kitchen counter telling Dad my dreams."

"You must have been about four then," says Mom.

I used to smell breakfast cooking as I came downstairs every morning. Dad would be making toast and eggs. I could feel the heat from the woodstove. Steller's jays would be watching Dad through the windows. "Good morning, Bubbo," he'd say. "Good dreams last night?" He'd lift me onto the counter, and we'd talk until it was time for my mom and baby sister to wake up.

The dust from the dirt road makes clouds around our car. I think about the nights when Dad and I wrestled.

We'd kneel on the rug and glare at each other. When he came near me, I'd growl like a tiger. We called ourselves the Flying Aces because one of us was always flying over the top of the other as we wrestled.

"You win some, you lose some," Dad would say at the end of a game. But, just as I was walking away, he'd tackle me and we'd wrestle one more time. Then he would make up stories about the famous Flying Aces and all the places they had been.

By the time we reach the bottom of the road, my sister is asleep. Her head bumps from the car seat onto my shoulder and back again.

Mom tells me about the time Dad snuck into my candy on Halloween. "He ate it all up," she says, laughing, "and then he had to go to the store the next day to buy more for you."

I remind her of the time Dad was telling a story leaning back in an old chair. When he waved his arms, the chair fell apart, and he ended up on the floor.

It feels good to talk and laugh about the funny things Dad did.

Mom drives up the gravel road to our house. The fir trees bend over our car like a round green roof.

Dad and I used to hike behind these trees and into the woods. We called it bushwhacking. We made trails through the forest to the neighbor's pond. Dad showed me how to mark a path so I could find my way home. He taught me how to climb a rock hill by testing the rocks to see if they were strong enough to hold me.

"If you're climbing and a rock slips," he told me, "you could fall so suddenly you wouldn't even know what happened."

At the pond, we'd skip rocks in the water. I would look for flat stones, because Dad said they skipped better. Once, Dad made a rock jump six times before it sank to the bottom.

Mom carries my sister to her room. A little bit of sand falls each time she takes a step. "I'll be outside," I call upstairs. Out on the front porch I watch the mourning doves fly into the tall spruce by the tree house.

At the end of the day, Dad would drive up and park his big green truck by that tree. I used to watch him come up the long walkway to the house. "Check my pockets, Bubbo," he'd say as he opened the door. I'd find a piece of candy, a toy, or a feather he had picked up. My sister's surprise would be hidden in Dad's fist because she was too little to reach his pockets.

For a while, after Dad died, I thought he would still come home for dinner like he always had. He would park his truck by the tree and come up the walkway with a surprise. I didn't want to believe that I wouldn't see him again.

I didn't want to believe that Dad had died. His heart stopped beating, and it couldn't be fixed. It stopped so suddenly, he didn't know what happened.

At the hospital Mom told me, "A terrible thing has happened. Dad has died."

I felt like I was tumbling and falling down a hill. I felt cold, like my body had turned to ice. I thought maybe I was dreaming.

The days passed slowly then. I felt a great sadness digging down inside of me.

Some days I felt so angry I wanted to hit someone. It was like a big cloudburst was in my head and thunder and lightning were around my heart.

Sometimes I would sit, wearing Dad's jacket, and wonder where he was. I thought about rolling down the sand dunes with him and watching pelicans fly over the wave tops. I wished I could change everything and have things the way they used to be.

Mom comes out on the porch to sit beside me. "Lots of memories?" she asks. I nod and lay my head on her lap.

I look up at her. She looks like she is remembering, too. "What are you thinking?" I ask.

"I was thinking of last Christmas without Dad," she says.

The week before Christmas, Mom took my sister and me to the city. We saw a Christmas tree taller than our house. Next to the tree was a plaque as big as me. It was painted white and had lots of names on it. Dad's name was there, and my mom and I touched the letters with our fingers.

"Will a lot of people remember Dad?" I asked her.

"Yes," she said, "a lot of people will remember Dad."

I think of Dad every day, and I'm glad other people think of him, too.

We go into the house to set the table for dinner.

"Let's make dinner special tonight," Mom says. "We'll light candles and play Dad's favorite music."

My sister comes downstairs holding her blanket balled up in her arms like a doll. She lies on the couch and watches me.

I look at the box that used to hold Dad's ashes. On the side is a carving that looks like wheat. His friends made the box out of wood. I know Dad would like how smooth it is. If he were here, he would run his hands over it and say, "Just feel that wood."

Above the box is a picture of Dad holding me when I was a baby. It was a long time before I could look at that picture and not feel sad. But one day I looked at Dad's face and it made me smile.

Soon after that, I looked at Dad's jacket and didn't feel a big hole in my stomach. I even took out his jackknife the other day, and Mom helped me clean all the blades.

Most of the time now, I can skip rocks and watch them skim over the water without feeling sad.

I'm not sure how it happened, but it's been a long time since I felt the big cloudburst in my head.

"I think Dad would like this dinner," I tell Mom.

"I'm sure he would," she answers.

"And I know he'd like the way I can climb the hills like a mountain goat," I add.

"And he'd like hearing a baseball crack against your bat," she says.

"I like flying in the air," my sister says. My mom and I laugh. My sister remembers being thrown in the air by Dad because we've told her the story so many times.

Mom lights the candles. "Remember last Christmas morning?" she asks.

We took some of Dad's ashes to the ocean, and each of us threw a handful into the waves. "I told you we should put Dad's ashes in all the places he loved," I answer.

"Now there's a part of Dad in the mountains, in the sea, in the river, even under the trees in the garden." She smiled. "And that makes me feel happy."

"There's a part of Dad in us, too," I say.

"You know," I tell her as I put on one of Dad's cello records, "it's like when Dad died, he split into a thousand pieces so he could be with all the people he loved. And I'm glad some of the pieces are with me."